Guess what I'll be

illustrated by **Anni Axworthy**

WALKER BOOKS
AND SUBSIDIARIES
LONDON • BOSTON • SYDNEY

D1420843

What will I be?

This is me.
I'm called a tadpole.

One day I'll have four webby feet.

Big bulging eyes.

And I'll eat beetles, flies and worms.

Frogs live on
the land and in
the water.

What will I be?

This is me.
I'm called a chick.

One day I'll have
two long skinny legs.

Bright pink
feathers.

And a very
large hooked
beak.

Flamingos turn pink
because they eat so
many pink prawns.

What will I be?

This is me. I'm called a caterpillar.

One day I'll have
long wavy feelers
called antennae.

And big
colourful wings.

And I'll fly
from flower to flower.

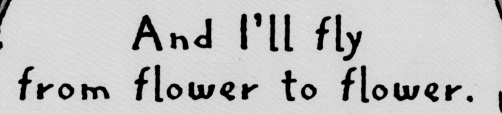

Butterflies like nectar, the sugary food in flowers.

What will I be?

This is me.
I'm called a calf.

One day I'll have
two long tusks.

Wrinkly
brown skin.

And I'll swim in the sea.

Walruses live in large
groups called herds.

What will I be?

This is me. I'm called a grub.

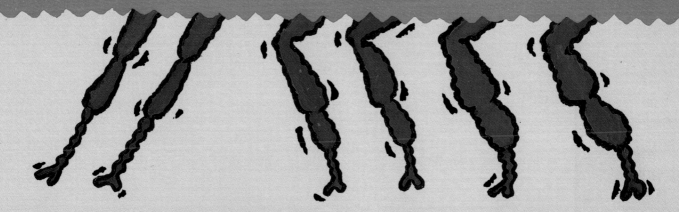

One day I'll have six busy legs.

A stripy body.

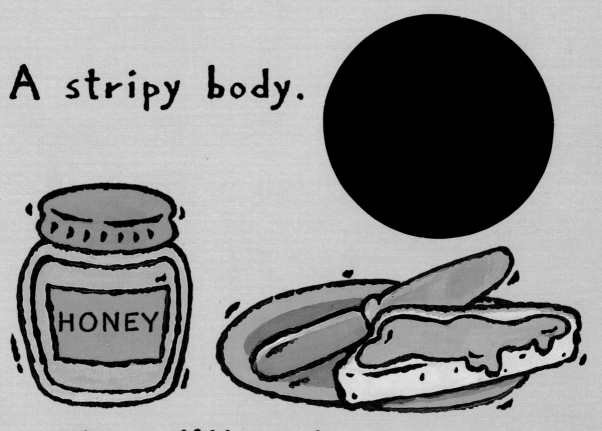

And I'll make honey.

Bees make honey
to feed their babies.

Grub
to...flamingo?

Tadpole
to...butterfly?

Calf
to...frog?

First published 1998 by Walker Books Ltd
87 Vauxhall Walk, London SE11 5HJ

2 4 6 8 10 9 7 5 3 1

Series concept and design by Louise Jackson

Words by Louise Jackson and Paul Harrison

Wildlife consultant: Martin Jenkins

This book has been typeset in Joe Overweight.

Printed in Singapore

British Library Cataloguing in Publication Data
A catalogue record for this book is available
from the British Library.

ISBN 0-7445-6214-7